2

Myths and legends

Roderick Hunt

Illustrated by
Victor Ambrus
Robert Ayton   Allan Curless
Sarah De'Ath   Liza Jensen
Peter Kesteven
Brian Melling   Roger Payne
Joanna Troughton
Michael Whittlesea
Joe Wright

Oxford University Press

Contents

Oxford University Press, Great Clarendon Street, Oxford OX2 6DP
© Roderick Hunt 1981
Published 1981. Reprinted 1983, 1984, 1988, 1989, 1992, 1994, 1997
Filmset by Tradespools Ltd, Frome, Somerset. Printed in Malaysia

Thomas

Janet and Tam Lin lived happily together.
Tam Lin loved Janet deeply
    for she had saved him from the Elfin Queen.
Janet loved Tam Lin for his good looks
    and his gentle smiling eyes.
But she never forgot the Elfin Queen's warning.
'If a child is ever born to you.
    I shall try to win him for my own.'

It was not long before Janet and Tam Lin
    had a fine bonny son.
He had Tam Lin's good looks
    and Janet's kind, sweet ways.
They called their son Thomas.

Thomas grew into a strong, handsome boy.
Janet never let him out of her sight.
One day Tam Lin said to Janet,
    'It is not good for Thomas
        to stay so close to you.
    He must grow up like other boys.
    He must learn to ride and hunt.
    Let him ride with me today.
    I will take good care of him.'

And so Tam Lin took Thomas out
    to hunt deer in the woods.
Tam Lin made sure that Thomas rode
    close to him all the time.
No one knew better than Tam Lin
    the magic powers of the Elfin Queen.
On the way home, a bitter wind sprang up.
    and a great rain storm began.
'We cannot ride on in this,'
    shouted Tam Lin.
    'Let's shelter in that cottage ahead.'

An old woman lived in the cottage.
She bade them come in
    to sit by her bright warm fire.
She gave them some hot broth.
Then she dried Thomas's wet clothes.
'Why, the boy is chilled to the bone,'
    cried the old woman.
    'Put this rug round him.'
Tam Lin did not notice that the rug
    was the skin of a white stag.
Thomas found the skin soothing and warm.
It made him feel safe and sleepy.
'Why, the boy is tired out.
    Let him sleep until the rain stops,'
        said the old woman.
'You are very kind,' Tam Lin told her.

As Thomas slept, he had a dream.
He saw in it a beautiful white stag.
'Follow me! Follow me!' it called.
Thomas wanted to go with the white stag
    more than he had ever wanted anything.
'I'm coming,' he called, 'I'm coming.'
In his dream he followed the stag.
It led him to an enchanted place.
It seemed very beautiful.
'Come along, Thomas. Come along.'
And he awoke to hear Tam Lin
    saying it was time to go home.

How was Tam Lin to know
    the old woman was the Elfin Queen?
How was he to know the white skin
    of the stag had cast a spell on Thomas?

Back at home Janet's eyes were red.
'Why have you been so long?' she wept.
    'I was afraid for Thomas.'
Tam Lin held Janet close to him.
'We had to shelter from the storm.
    We are quite safe now,' he said.
'But we have had no storm!' cried Janet.
    'It has been fine and warm all day.'
Her words made Tam Lin's heart grow cold.
He ran to Thomas and held his arms.
'Thomas,' he said slowly,
    'did you dream when you fell asleep
        in the old woman's cottage?'
But Thomas's dream had been elfin magic.
'Did I fall asleep?' he said.
    'I don't remember.'

Now they were both afraid for Thomas.
Yet as the days went by,
   their fears came to nothing.
The days turned into weeks.
The weeks turned into months
   and the months turned into a year.
Thomas grew a little bigger.
Janet and Tam Lin almost forgot
   about the old woman in the cottage.

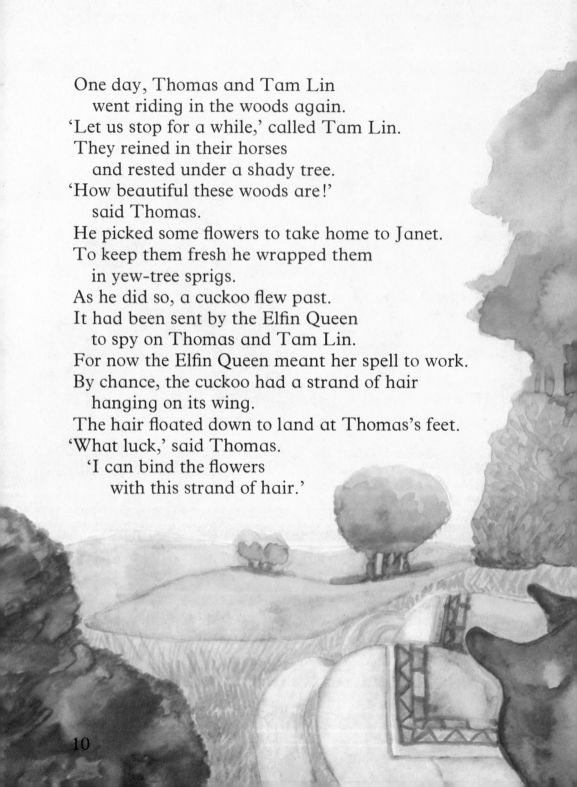

One day, Thomas and Tam Lin
    went riding in the woods again.
'Let us stop for a while,' called Tam Lin.
They reined in their horses
    and rested under a shady tree.
'How beautiful these woods are!'
    said Thomas.
He picked some flowers to take home to Janet.
To keep them fresh he wrapped them
    in yew-tree sprigs.
As he did so, a cuckoo flew past.
It had been sent by the Elfin Queen
    to spy on Thomas and Tam Lin.
For now the Elfin Queen meant her spell to work.
By chance, the cuckoo had a strand of hair
    hanging on its wing.
The hair floated down to land at Thomas's feet.
'What luck,' said Thomas.
    'I can bind the flowers
        with this strand of hair.'

Thomas pushed the flowers into his coat.
'Let us ride on,' he called to Tam Lin.
As he spoke he felt a strange feeling.
He seemed to hear a voice calling him.
'Follow me! Follow me!'
Among the trees he saw the white stag.
He knew he had to follow it.
The stag leapt away, and Thomas
    spurred his horse after it.
'I'm coming,' he called, 'I'm coming.'
On and on they sped like the wind.
Tam Lin was left far behind.
Over hills and dales they went.
They seemed to fly in the air.
Then at last they came to a mountain.
In the side was an open door.
The white stag leapt inside.
Thomas followed and the door in the mountain
    crashed shut behind them.

Thomas was in an enchanted place.
It was so lovely it took his breath away.
It glowed in a pale silvery light
    and silvery music played.
In front of Thomas was the Elfin Queen.
She wove her spell round him
    like a silver net.
She seemed to him so beautiful,
    he wanted to stay with her for ever.
She gave him wine in a golden cup
    and food on silver plates.
Then Thomas took the flowers from his coat
    to give to the Elfin Queen.

The Elfin Queen screamed in terror.
Sprigs of the yew tree tied with her own hair!
At once the spell was broken.
She fell to the floor choking and gasping.
'Go!' she cried. 'Go Thomas, son of Tam Lin!
    How did you learn such magic?
    Go! For I will never trouble you again.'
Then Thomas found himself
    alone on the outside of the mountain.
He could see no sign
    of the enchanted door.

Thomas quickly made his way home.
There he found Janet and Tam Lin.
He greeted them with great joy
   and told them of the enchanted mountain.
Then he saw sadness in Janet's face.
'Not all the spell was broken,' she said.
'You see, Thomas,' said Tam Lin,
   'the Elfin Queen meant to keep you forever.
   You have been gone from us for five years.'

How the wren became king

All the birds held a meeting.
They wanted to choose a king.
But they could not agree
   how the choice was to be made.
'Beauty is what we want in a king,'
   said the peacock.
'Well I say we need dignity,' said the owl.
   Let us see who looks wisest.'
'Or who talks the best,' said the parrot.

16

Then the eagle spoke.
'What makes us what we are?
    Why, the power of flying.
    We must choose as our king
        the bird that can fly highest.'
In the end, the eagle had the last word.
All the birds got ready to try
    the test proposed by the eagle.
At a signal, the birds flew up.
Each tried to fly as high as he could.
But the eagle rose above them all.
Way, way up he went, into the blue sky.
At last the eagle could go no higher.
All the time, however, the little wren
    had been perching on the eagle's back.
Of course it was not tired.
It took off and flew up
    even higher than the eagle.

To the disgust of all the birds,
    the little wren became king.

Legends about birds

There are many legends about the wren.
It is one of the best known
   of small British birds.
There is a custom called Hunting the Wren,
It dates back hundreds of years.
It takes place between Boxing Day (St. Stephen's Day)
   and Twelfth Night (January 6th).
The wren was said to bring a bad winter.
People used to hunt and kill one
   then carry it from house to house.
It was hoped that this would bring good luck.
Even today the custom takes place
   but of course only dummy wrens are used.

The robin is a well-loved bird
    with its red breast and friendly ways.
Many people think that the wren
    is the hen-bird of the robin.
This is not true.
It is said to be bad luck to kill a robin
    or steal its eggs.
There are many legends about its red breast.
One says that it helped mankind
    by bringing fire to Earth.
In doing so, it scorched its feathers red.

There is a legend about the kingfisher.
Noah is said to have sent one with the dove
    to search for dry land after the flood.
The kingfisher flew so high, its feathers
    were turned orange by the sun
        and blue by the sky.

19

There are many stories about the raven.
In some parts of Britain, people said
    they were the Devil's birds.
But in Wales, ravens were regarded
    as royal birds.
One legend says that King Arthur
    turned into one.
No birds in the world are more looked after
    than the ravens in the Tower of London.
Legend says that if they vanish
    Britain will have a terrible disaster.

In many places there are stories
  about a flock of birds
    called the Seven Whistlers.
They whistle sadly as they fly past.
It is said that there are only six birds
  and they are searching for the seventh.
When they find it, the world will end.

People used to be afraid of owls.
If one hooted near a house
  it was a sign of very bad luck.
It meant bad news was on the way.
If a baby was born as an owl hooted
  the child would have an unlucky life.

21

The magic box

No one was as happy as Patrick
   and his pretty wife, Mary.
They lived on a small farm
   with their three fine children.
Mary looked after the farmhouse.
She kept it neat and tidy.
It shone like a new pin.
Patrick looked after the farm.
He worked in the fields
   and he kept cows and sheep.

Their three children worked hard too.
The oldest milked the cow
    and made the butter.
The next fed their fine white pig
    and kept its sty clean.
The youngest fed the chickens
    and looked for brown eggs
        in the yellow straw.

23

One day there was a terrible storm.
There had never been a storm like it.
The wind howled and the rain beat down.
It seemed as if it was the end of the world.

At last the storm stopped.
Patrick and Mary and the children
    looked at the farm in dismay.
The barn had blown away
    and all the chickens had gone with it.
The cows and sheep had wandered off.
They could not be found anywhere.
The rain had washed the rich earth away
    from all the fields.
All that was left was stone and clay.
'I shall never be able to grow anything
    in this poor ground,' cried Patrick.

At the bottom of the valley
  lived Mean McPhee and his ten lazy sons.
After the storm was over
  they looked over their farm.
A barn had been blown into their yard.
Some cows and sheep had wandered
  into their meadow.
There were chickens on the farmhouse roof.
Some fine, rich earth had washed
  on to Mean McPhee's fields.
McPhee rubbed his hands.
'Well boys,' he said, 'that storm
  has done us some good.'

'You mean we're going to keep the barn
    and the animals and the earth?'
        asked the ten lazy sons.
'Sure we are,' said Mean McPhee,
    'unless you want to put them on a barrow
        and go and see whose they are.'
'Not us,' said the ten lazy sons.

The next day, Patrick went down the valley
    to call on Mean McPhee.
McPhee and his ten lazy sons
    were leaning on their farm gate.
Patrick told them about his barn,
    his animals and his good, rich earth.
'Did the storm blow them here?' he asked.
Mean McPhee bunched his hand into a fist.
His ten big, lazy sons did the same.
'We got nothing in the storm,'
    said McPhee, 'did we lads?'
'Not us,' said the ten lazy sons.

Patrick, Mary and their three children
   grew poorer and poorer.
They had to kill their fine, white pig.
All they had to eat was bacon
   and a few turnips.
'The bacon won't last for ever,'
   said Mary, 'then what shall we do?'
One day they sat down to supper.
There was a knock on the door.
It was a tiny old man.
He looked thin and frail.
A puff of wind would almost blow him away.
'It is dark outside and I'm lost,'
   said the old man in a thin voice.
   'Will you put me up for the night?'
'Come in and warm yourself,' said Patrick.
   'We haven't much to eat,
      but you are welcome to share it with us.'

The old man sat by the fire.
Mary gave him some bacon.
He ate it hungrily.
Mary gave him some more.
At last he had eaten every scrap.
Then he fell fast asleep in the chair.
The family looked at him in dismay.
'What a strange old man,' said Mary.
   'He can't have known we've no more food.'
She put a rug over him to keep him warm.
Then all the family went to bed.

The next morning,
   they found the old man had gone.
He had folded the rug neatly.
On top of it was a small wooden box.
'He didn't stay to thank us,' said Patrick.
   'Perhaps he left this box for us.'
He read out some writing on the lid:
      'Gold from the mountains
       Stones from the sea.
       Whatever I deserve
       Now give to me.'
At once the lid of the box flew open
   and gold coins poured on to the floor.
'A magic box!' shouted Patrick.
He and Mary jumped up and down.
They danced a jig round and round
   and laughed and laughed.
'It will provide us with all we need,
but we must not be lazy or greedy.
We must only use the box
   when we really need it,' said Patrick.

So Patrick, Mary and the children
   were happy once again.
They had money to buy more animals.
Patrick put up a new barn.
Mary had a new dress.
The children had new shoes.

Mean McPhee passed Patrick's farm one day.
'How can Patrick be so well off?' he wondered.
He crept up and peered in the window.
At that very moment,
  Patrick was holding the magic box.
      'Gold from the mountains
      Stones from the sea.
      Whatever I deserve
      Now give to me.'
McPhee saw the coins pour out of the box.
His eyes almost popped out of his head.
'I'll come back tonight and steal that box,'
  said McPhee, meanly.

That night, McPhee crept back
    and stole the magic box.
He rushed back to his farm
    and shut himself in his kitchen.
Then he said aloud:
        'Gold from the mountain
        Stones from the sea.
        Whatever I deserve
        Now give to me.'
At once the lid of the box flew open.
Stones began to pour out of it.
They poured on to the floor
    and McPhee couldn't stop them.
Soon they filled the kitchen,
    and then the whole house.

Suddenly the house began to rise up
  on the pile of stones.
'Stop! Stop!' shouted McPhee,
  but the house went on up and up.
The ten lazy sons were flung out of bed.
Soon the house was perched on the top
  of a huge pile of stones.
There it swayed from side to side,
  like a great see-saw.

McPhee clung to the roof
   and looked down to the ground.
Below him stood a tiny old man.
'Help! Help!' wailed Mean McPhee.
   'Do something, please!'
'Do you promise to give back
   what does not belong to you?'
    called the little old man.
'Anything,' sobbed Mean McPhee.

At once the pile of stones
    turned into a pile of rich earth.
The house slid gently back to the ground.
'Now,' said the little old man.
    'First give me back the magic box.
    Then take back all that belongs
        to the farm at the top of the valley.'
McPhee gave the box to the old man.
'We can take back all the animals.
    We can take back the barn.
    But how can we take back the earth?'
The old man waved his hand in the air.
At once there were eleven barrows
    and eleven spades by the pile of earth.
Suddenly McPhee knew that the old man
    was one of the Little People.
He handed each of his ten lazy sons
    a spade and gave each one a barrow
'Get shovelling, boys,' he said.

Aesop the Greek

Aesop, the wonderful story teller,
  was born a slave.
There is a legend about Aesop.
Not only was he very, very ugly,
  he grew up unable to speak.
He could only stammer and grunt.
Really Aesop was clever.
He was gentle and kind-hearted,
  but people took him for a fool.
He was often badly treated by his master
  and the other slaves.

One day some travellers were lost.
They saw Aesop working in the fields.
They called out to ask him the way.
Then they saw his strange, ugly looks
    and heard his odd stammers and grunts.
'This poor chap can't help us,' said one.
    'He can't even talk.'
But in the end, Aesop made them
    understand him.
First he made them rest in the shade,
    for it was a very hot day.
Then he gave them food and a cool drink.
At last, he made them follow him
    until they found their path again.

Aesop would not take anything
    for helping the strangers.
So the good people prayed to the gods
    to reward Aesop in some way.
Almost at once Aesop felt very, very tired.
He rested under a tree and fell asleep.
In his dream he saw Athene,
    the goddess of wisdom.
Athene gave Aesop the power to speak.
'However ugly you look,' she told him,
    'the gift of wisdom will be yours.
        People will come to love and respect you.'

Aesop woke with a start.
His dream had started to come true!
He had been given the gift of speech.
Aesop the slave became a famous
    and important man.
The stories he told are called fables.
Each fable has a lesson for us to learn.
Aesop wrote his fables two and a half
    thousand years ago.
People still read them, even today.

One of Aesop's fables

A dog once walked along a plank
   over a deep stream.
In his mouth was a piece of meat.
Half-way across the plank
   he saw his reflection in the water.
Thinking it was another dog,
   he tried to snatch the meat from it.
This made him open his mouth
   and he dropped the meat into the stream.

Be content with what you have.
If you try to steal what others have,
   you will lose more than you gain.

AESOP

The boy who cried wolf

'I'm bored looking after silly old sheep,'
  said the shepherd boy.
  'All they do is munch grass and bleat at me.
  Well, if I can't stir the sheep
    I can stir the villagers.'
So the boy shouted, 'Wolf! Wolf!'
  at the top of his voice.
The men from the village rushed up the hill
  with sticks and axes.
'Where's the wolf?' they cried.
'Ha! Ha! That fooled you,' called the boy.
The villagers went away,
  thankful the boy had not been attacked.

After this the boy shouted, 'Wolf!'
  several times.
Each time the men ran up the hill.
But the boy had only been joking.

At last a wolf really did come.
The boy cried 'Wolf! Wolf!' in terror.
This time no one came from the village.
They were tired of his silly joke.
And so the wolf attacked the sheep
   and killed one after the other.

It is hard to believe a liar
   even when he tells the truth for once.

AESOP

The King's choice

Long, long ago in a far-off land
  there lived a wise old King.
The King had no children of his own
  and he longed to have a son.
Imagine how pleased he was
  when, one day, the Queen told him
  he was soon to be a father.
'This is wonderful news,' he said.
  'The baby is sure to be a boy.
  Now we will have a son to be king
  when I grow too old for the job.'

The King could hardly wait
    for the baby to be born.
'I will soon be the father of a son,'
    he said to his Prime Minister.
    'Go out and buy some boxing-gloves,
        football-boots and roller-skates.
    Get a bow and arrow set made for him.
    Oh, and buy a few marbles while you're at it'.
'But what if we have a baby girl?'
    asked the Queen gently.
'Don't be silly, my dear,' said the King.
    'I know we're going to have a boy.'

At last the great day came.
The King paced up and down
   outside the Queen's chamber.
All the ministers and wise men
   paced up and down, too.
'I dread to think what will happen
   if the Queen has a baby girl,'
      muttered the Prime Minister.

46

Then came the lusty cries of a baby
    from the Queen's chamber.
'The baby has been born,' breathed the King,
    'but goodness what a noise it makes!'
The door of the Queen's chamber opened.
The ministers held their breath.
The wise men crossed their fingers.
A lady-in-waiting stood at the door
    with a little white bundle in her arms.
'Is it a son?' asked the King, at once.
No, Your Majesty,' said the lady-in-waiting.

Behind her stood two more ladies-in-waiting.
Each had a little white bundle in her arms.
'You don't just have a son, Your Majesty,
    you have three sons!'
'Three sons!' gasped the King.
    'You mean I have trip-ups?'
'Not *tripups*, Your Majesty, *triplets*,'
    said the Prime Minister wisely.
His words were wasted, for the King's knees bent
    and he fainted on the floor.

As soon as the King came round,
 he was overjoyed to have three sons.
'See what fine boys they are,' he said,
 and he passed them from wise man to minister
  and from minister to wise man.
'But, Your Majesty,' asked the Prime Minister,
 'which of them will be king one day?'
'Why, the oldest of course,' said the King.
 'The one who was born first.'
'And which one is that?' asked the Prime Minister.
The King scratched his head.
In all the excitement of passing them round,
 no one knew which baby was which.
And that was how the trouble started.

Year by year, the King watched his sons grow up.
He was never sure from one day to the next
    which of them should be king.
The three sons were very different indeed.
One son was very big and strong.
He was bold and daring in a fight.
He spent most of his time
    fighting with the King's knights.
None of them could beat him.
'He would be a good king
    if it came to a battle,' said the old King
        to his wise men.
Another son was very, very clever.
He was sharp and quick with his brain.
He spent most of his time
    arguing with the wise men.
None of them could catch him out.
'He would be a good king
    at making new laws and things,' said the old King
        to his ministers.
The third son wasn't very strong
    and he wasn't very clever.
He didn't like fighting
    and he didn't like arguing.
'He's really quite ordinary,' said the King
    to his ministers and wise men.
    'He even likes to spend his time
        talking to ordinary people.
    He's not at all like his brothers.
    I'm not at all sure he would be
        good at anything, much,' he added.

At last, the King called together
    all his wise men and ministers.
They sat arguing for hours and hours.
They could still not agree
    which son would be the best king.
'There's only one thing to be done.
    We shall have to use magic,' said the King.
    'Go out and find a magician
        and make sure he knows what he's doing.'

After many days the ministers and wise men
    came back with an old, old man.
'His name is Mantin, Your Majesty,' they said.
    'He is the best magician in the land.'
Mantin told the King to call the three sons.
Then he looked them up and down.
At last he took three small silver bottles
    from the pocket of his robe.
'In these bottles is a magic drink,' he said.
    'The magic will only last for a day
        but it will increase your powers
            one hundred times.'
'You mean I will be a hundred times stronger
    for one whole day?' said the strong son.
'Or that I will be a hundred times cleverer?'
    said the clever son.
'Or that I will be a hundred times
    a better person?' said the other son.
'Each of you will have a day to prove
    you are worthy to be the king,' said Mantin.
    'Let us begin the test at once.'

'Then I will go first,' cried the strong son.
He drank the contents of the bottle
   in one enormous gulp.
At once, he was a hundred times stronger.
With a great cry he ran into the forest.
He pulled a hundred oak trees
   from the ground and snapped their branches,
      just to prove how strong he was.

Then he rushed to the mountains
and sped back with huge blocks of stone.
He built a tall stone tower
on the edge of the forest.
By the end of the day it was complete.
'No other kingdom has a tower like this,'
he cried.
'This will prove to everyone
what a good king I would make.'

On the next day, the clever son
    opened his silver bottle.
He drank the magic contents in one gulp.
With a great cry he ran down to the lake.
He killed a hundred geese
    and pulled out the feathers for quill pens.
Then he rushed to his room.
'Bring me all the writing paper
    in the land,' he told the wise men.

Then he sat down and did a huge sum.
The sum filled up a thousand books,
    each with a thousand pages.
By the end of the day he cried,
    'I can tell you how heavy the world is.
    It is ten thousand million million
        million tons.
    No man has ever worked that out.
    That will prove to everyone
        what a good king I would make.'

The third day was the last son's turn.
He put the silver bottle to his lips.
But no one saw that he only took
   a tiny, tiny sip.
Then he slipped away before anyone
   had time to see him go.
At the end of the day, he came back
   as quietly as he had gone.
He knelt at the old King's feet.
'I took only a sip of the magic drink,' he said.
   'It made me twice the man I am.
    I took the geese my clever brother killed,
     and gave them to the poor to eat.
    I took the trees my strong brother snapped,
     and gave them away for firewood.
    Then I took the paper from my clever
     brother's sum, and gave it to the children
      to paint on.'

'Last of all, I took the children
  to the tower my strong brother built.
  I let them climb and play on it
    for that is all the use it is.
  I still have the magic drink.
  If I am made king, there will be many times
    I shall need to be twice the man I am.'

Which son do you think
  became king?

The terror of Gubbio

The sun began to set.
In the small town of Gubbio,
   people called their children inside.
Then they shut their windows
   and locked their doors.
Soon there was no one about.
The streets were silent.
Fear hung over the town.

That night a stranger came to the town.
He walked down the empty streets.
He felt eyes peering at him
    from every window.
He sensed the fear everywhere.
A window in one of the houses opened.
A man shouted at the stranger.
'Are you mad?' he called.
    'It will soon be on the prowl.
    Get inside before it's too late.'
The stranger smiled.
'I am a man of God,' he said.
    'What is this evil thing
        you all fear so much?'
'You *must* be a stranger,' said the man.
    'Have you not heard?
    A savage wolf prowls our streets.
    It comes from the woods
        outside our town.
    It attacks soon after dark.
    No one is safe from it.
    Get inside, quickly.'

The stranger smiled again.
'This wolf you speak of,' he said.
   'Is it big and old?
   Does it have a limp?'
'So you *have* seen it?' said the man.
'No,' said the stranger,
   'but I know and love God's creatures,
      even this old, lone wolf.
   It is not savage or evil.
   It is old and lame.
   Its pack has deserted it.
   That is why it hunts in your town.
   It does not mean any harm.'
The man slammed the window shut.
'Tell that to the wolf
   as its teeth close round your throat,'
      he muttered.

The next morning the news
   was all over the town.
The stranger was in the market square.
The wolf was sitting at his feet.
'They say he's tamed it!'
   cried the women.
'We'll believe that when we see it,'
   shouted the men.

They picked up sticks and axes
  and made their way to the square.
It was true. There sat the stranger
  and the savage wolf.
'Are you mad?' the men shouted.
'Do not be afraid,' the stranger called.
  'The wolf will not attack you.
  See, I can hold my wrist in its jaws
    quite safely.
  Give the wolf food each day
    and it will no longer harm you.'

The stranger's words came true.
The people did leave food out.
The wolf no longer prowled at night.
People no longer went in fear of the wolf.
Soon they forgot it was a wild animal.
It seemed gentle and content.
Before long, the savage wolf became a friend
　　to everyone in the town.
Even the children played with it.

The stranger was Saint Francis.
He lived in Italy
　　over seven hundred years ago.
He loved all God's creatures.
He tried to show other people
　　how to love them too.
Saint Francis of Assisi is known as
　　the patron saint of animals.

Rajeb's reward

There was once a young man called Rajeb.
He lived in a far-off town
    in a far-off country.
Rajeb was not rich but he was not poor.
His father had left him two thousand dinars.
'It is not a lot of money,' said Rajeb,
    'but it will give me a start.
    I can pay for some goods with it.
    Then I can buy a little stall
        in the market-place.
    I will work hard on my stall.
    Then one day I may have a small shop.
    Perhaps I will even end up with a big shop
        in a rich part of town.'

One hot day, Rajeb passed the gateway
of a well-to-do house.
From the courtyard came the sound
of splashing water.
Rajeb longed for a cool drink.
He gazed into the shady courtyard.
There he saw a young girl.
She had pulled aside her veil
to drink the clear, cold water.
Her face was so beautiful,
Rajeb at once fell in love with her.
The girl saw Rajeb staring at her.
She pulled the veil back over her face
and ran into the house.

Rajeb went home in a daze.
He could think of nothing but the beautiful girl.
She was on his mind every day.
He forgot all about his plan
    to use the two thousand dinars.
All he wanted to do was to
    marry the beautiful girl.
He found out that she was called Ameera.
Not only was she beautiful,
    she was kind and gentle, too.

At last Rajeb made up his mind
    to go boldly to Ameera's house.
There he spoke to her father.
  'I am in love with Ameera,' he said,
      'and wish to marry her.'
The father saw that Rajeb was strong
    and good-looking.
He would be a good husband for Ameera.
'Yes,' he said, 'you may marry her.
    But first you must be rich.
    You must bring me five thousand dinars.'

'Come back within a week,'
    said the father.
    'Other men also wish to marry Ameera.
    She is very beautiful.
    She will indeed make a good wife.'
Poor Rajeb!
How could he ever find
    such a big dowry for Ameera?
Back in his room he counted
    his two thousand dinars
        again and again.
But however hard he tried,
    he could not make them any more.
Suddenly Rajeb had an idea.
'My uncle Jousof is said to be rich.
    I have not seen him for many years
        and he lives a long way away.
    All the same, I will pay him a visit.
    Perhaps he will lend me the money
        for Ameera's dowry.'

So Rajeb set off, and in two days
    he came to the little town.
There he asked some boys
    for the house of his uncle,
        the rich Jousof.
'The *rich* Jousof!' yelled the boys.
    'That's a good one.
    You mean the old miser, Jousof.
    He says he hasn't a penny to his name
        and he lives like a beggar.'

Rajeb's heart sank.
Even so, he asked the boys
   to take him to his uncle.
There he found an old man
   in a poor, broken-down house.

At first, the old man almost shut the door
   in Rajeb's face.
'Uncle! Uncle! It is me, Rajeb,
   your sister's son.
   I have come a long way to see you,'

At last, Jousof let Rajeb in.
Inside, the house was poor and dirty.
Rajeb had to sit on the floor.
   'How is it that my rich uncle
       can live like this?' he wondered.
The old man knew what Rajeb was thinking.

'I am almost a beggar,' he sniffed.
    No one is poorer than I.
    I hope you have not come all this way
        to ask for money.
    I have none to give you.'
Then Rajeb told his uncle about his
    love for Ameera.
He hoped his words would soften
    the old man's heart.
'I can lend you nothing,' said Jousof,
    'so don't ask me again.'

Sadly Rajeb got up to go,
   but the old man stopped him.
'Now you are here,' he said,
  'you can do me a good turn.
  I have an old donkey behind the house.
  He is no good to me.
  Stay here, and in the morning
   you can help me sell him.
  You can make sure no one robs me
   in the market-place.'

Rajeb went outside to see the donkey.
He felt sorry for it.
  'You're just a bag of skin and bones.
  I'll go and buy you some oats,' he said.
The donkey looked at Rajeb with big, soft eyes.
Then he stamped on the ground
    three times with its hoof.
'I bet you could tell a story or two
    about Jousof,' Rajeb said.
  'And he's going to sell you in the morning.'

At the market the next day
   Rajeb felt even more sorry for the donkey.
No one wanted to buy it.
The only offer Jousof had
   was three hundred dinars.
'I won't sell him for so little,' said Jousof.
   'Come on, we'll take the donkey back home.'
The donkey looked at Rajeb
   with it's big soft eyes.
Rajeb knew that Jousof would just let
   the animal grow thinner and thinner.
He did not want the donkey to starve.
'I'll buy him, then!' cried Rajeb.
'I don't want to sell him now,'
   said the mean old man, craftily.
'I'll give you six hundred dinars,' said Rajeb.
   Cunning old Jousof shook his head.
'Eight hundred, then,' cried Rajeb.
'Give me one thousand dinars,' said Jousof greedily,
   'and the donkey is yours.'
'Done!' cried Rajeb, and the donkey was his.

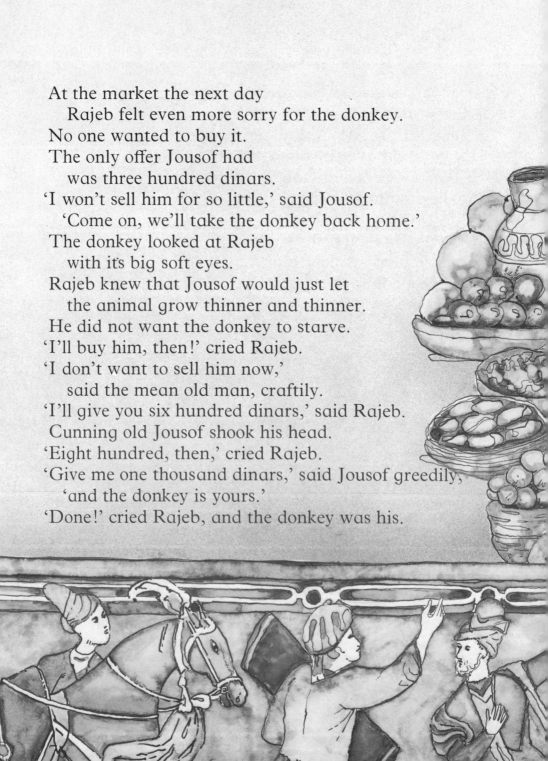

And so Rajeb said goodbye to Jousof
and took the donkey home.
'Well, I must be silly,' said Rajeb.
'I have spent half my money
on a skinny old donkey.
Now I shall never marry Ameera.'
The donkey looked at Rajeb
and rubbed its old head against him.

77

Now one day, some news came to Rajeb.
His Uncle Jousof had died.
'Well, he was a mean old man,' said Rajeb,
    'but I had better go and see to his house
        and sort out his things.'

Rajeb rode the donkey back to Jousof's.
The donkey ran almost all the way.
'You seem keen to get there,' said Rajeb.
The donkey *was* keen.
He trotted round behind Jousof's house.
Then he stamped on the ground.
'What's up?' asked Rajeb,
    but the donkey went on stamping his hoof.
'He wants me to dig at that spot,'
    said Rajeb, and he ran to find a spade.
Rajeb dug down into the hard ground.
Suddenly the spade hit an iron box.
Rajeb dug it out and opened it.
Then he gasped in amazement.
It was full of silver and gold
    and sparkling gems.
Rajeb had never seen such riches.
'Oh Donkey! Thanks to you,
    I am a rich man,' cried Rajeb.
    'Take me home as fast as you can.
    I shall marry the beautiful Ameera.
    We shall live happily ever after.
    You shall live in comfort
        for the rest of your days.'
And that's just what they did.

The Devil's bridge

An old lady once lived in a little cottage
beside a deep, swirling river.
The only way to cross the river
was over a stone bridge.
But that was two miles away
down a steep rocky path.

Every week, the old lady went to the town
to sell her eggs at the market.
Every week, she had to make her way
down the steep rocky path,
to cross over the bridge.
It took the poor old lady all day
to walk to the town and back.
'If only there was a bridge over the river
near my cottage,' she moaned.
'Then I wouldn't have to walk so far
on my poor stiff old legs.'

As time went by, the old lady's legs
   grew stiffer and stiffer.
Every week she found it harder and harder
   to walk all the way to market.
One morning she woke up and felt
   stiff and sore in every joint.
'I shan't be able to go to town today,' she said.
   'I'm just too stiff to go
      down that rocky path to the bridge.'
She looked at the fresh brown eggs
   her hens had laid and she said,
   'I would give anything in the world
      for a bridge close to my cottage.'
No sooner had she said this than she saw
   a strange-looking man at her door.
The old lady could not see very well
   so she did not know it was the Devil.
'Good day, old woman,' said the Devil.
   'What would you give me to put a bridge
      over the river close to your cottage?'
The old woman still had no idea
   she was dealing with the Devil.
'I would give anything in the world,' she said.
   'No one could build a bridge
      across such a deep river.'
'Then will you promise to give me
   anything I ask, if I build it?'
      the Devil asked slyly.
'Gladly,' said the old lady.
   'But it is unkind of you to tease me.
   No man could build such a bridge.'

Suddenly, the Devil changed shape.
He became as big as a giant
    and flew up into the air.
Then he began to build the bridge.
The ground shook, the rocks cracked,
    the stones broke, the trees snapped.
There was a crashing, a smashing
    and a splashing.
Before you could count to ten
    there was a stone bridge over the river
        just as the old lady had wanted.

84

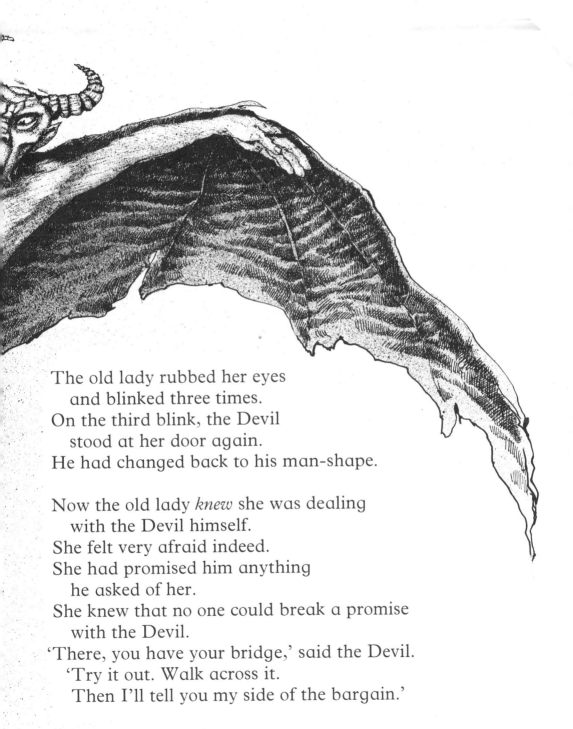

The old lady rubbed her eyes
  and blinked three times.
On the third blink, the Devil
  stood at her door again.
He had changed back to his man-shape.

Now the old lady *knew* she was dealing
  with the Devil himself.
She felt very afraid indeed.
She had promised him anything
  he asked of her.
She knew that no one could break a promise
  with the Devil.
'There, you have your bridge,' said the Devil.
  'Try it out. Walk across it.
  Then I'll tell you my side of the bargain.'

The old lady walked up to the bridge.
She was almost there when the Devil called,
  'The first living soul to cross the bridge
      will belong to me.'
The old lady did not want the Devil
    to have her soul.
But he began to come up behind her.
She knew he meant her to be the first
    to cross the bridge.

86

Suddenly, the old lady saw a way
   to trick the Devil.
Close to the bridge was her old
   black and white pig.
Now in her pocket was a sugary bun.
The old pig loved sugary buns.
It would do anything for one.
The Devil did not see the old lady
   show the bun to the pig.
But the greedy old pig rushed up
   to get it.
The Devil was knocked clean off his feet.
Before he had time to get up,
   the old lady threw the bun across the bridge.
The black and white pig ran after it.
It was the first living soul to cross over.

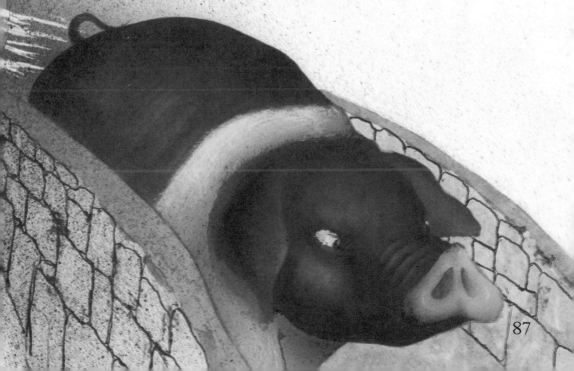

The Devil was angry at being tricked.
He became his giant shape again.
He flew up into the mountains.
He smashed up rocks and threw them
    down at the bridge.

The Devil missed every time.
But he filled the river with rocks.
And to this very day, the Devil's bridge
    stands over a rocky river.
As for the old lady, she lived in her house
    for many more years.
She was more than glad of the Devil's bridge.

Fisherman's folly

Two men once wanted to go fishing.
They went to a boatyard
    and hired a boat.

Then they found a good spot on the lake
    and started to fish.
It was such a good spot,
    they ended up with a boat
        full of fish.

'Make sure you mark the spot,'
said one of the men to the other.
'We'll come back and fish here again.'

When they got back, the first man said,
'Did you mark the spot as I told you?'
'Of course I did,' said the other man.
'I made a mark on the side of the boat.'
'You fool,' said the first man, crossly.
'They may not give us the same boat
next time we go fishing.'

He took the sun for a ride

'Show off! Show off!' shouted the boys.
They were jeering at a boy called Phaeton.
'I tell you I can run the fastest,'
    cried Phaeton angrily.
    'I can beat any one of you.'
'You'll be telling us you are the son
    of one of the gods, next,' said a boy.
'I can't help it if I'm good
    at everything,' said Phaeton.
'Oh go and boil your head!' the boys shouted.

Phaeton went to his mother, Clymene.
'Who is my father?' he asked.
    'Why have I never seen him?'
'Your father is Apollo,' said Clymene.
    'He is the god of the sun.'
Phaeton gasped.
'So I *am* the son of a god.
    No wonder I am good at everything!'
'You must not boast,' warned Clymene.
    'Your friends will not like you for it.'

But Phaeton could not help showing off.
He rushed to tell his friends
    that he really was the son of a god.
None of them would believe him.
'That's a good one,' they jeered.
    'Son of Apollo indeed.
    You'll show off once too often.
    You'd better go and *cool* your head now.'
Phaeton bit his lip.
'I'll teach them to jeer
    at the son of Apollo,' he vowed.
He ran home and spoke to his mother.
'Let me visit Apollo,' he begged.
    'He will help me prove I am his son.'
In the end, Clymene agreed.

At last Phaeton arrived
    at Apollo's glittering palace.
He made his way into the great hall
    just before dawn.
Apollo was seated on a golden throne.
On his head was a dazzling crown
    of sunrays.
The crown was so bright
    Phaeton had to shade his eyes.
'Who comes to the palace of the sun?'
    boomed Apollo.
'Sir, I am Phaeton, your son,
    sent here by my mother, Clymene.'
At once Apollo took off his sun-crown.
He held out his hands to welcome Phaeton.
'I am glad to see you, my son,' he said.
    'But why have you come to the sun palace?'
Phaeton told Apollo about his friends.
'They will not believe I am your son,' he said.
    'Help me to show them it is true.'

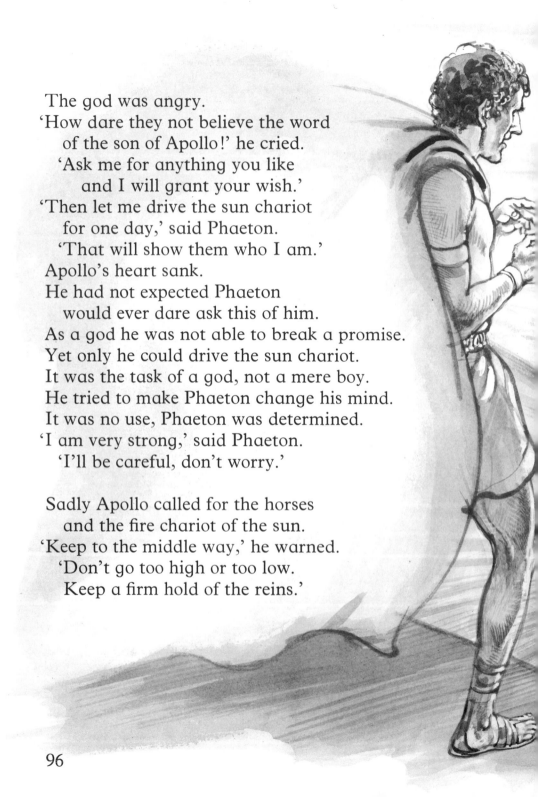

The god was angry.
'How dare they not believe the word
  of the son of Apollo!' he cried.
  'Ask me for anything you like
    and I will grant your wish.'
'Then let me drive the sun chariot
  for one day,' said Phaeton.
  'That will show them who I am.'
Apollo's heart sank.
He had not expected Phaeton
  would ever dare ask this of him.
As a god he was not able to break a promise.
Yet only he could drive the sun chariot.
It was the task of a god, not a mere boy.
He tried to make Phaeton change his mind.
It was no use, Phaeton was determined.
'I am very strong,' said Phaeton.
  'I'll be careful, don't worry.'

Sadly Apollo called for the horses
  and the fire chariot of the sun.
'Keep to the middle way,' he warned.
  'Don't go too high or too low.
    Keep a firm hold of the reins.'

Apollo called to Aurora, the dawn.
She threw open the gates of morning.
Phaeton sped the sun chariot forward.
The noise of the chariot drowned
   his father's warning.

Phaeton was too thrilled and excited
  to heed Apollo's words.
The Earth lay spread out below him.
'It won't hurt if I steer closer,' he thought.
  'I must let my friends see me.'
He jerked the reins, and the horses
  were no longer on the middle way.
Now the horses knew that Apollo's strong hands
  were not there to guide them.
Down, down towards the Earth they plunged.
They burned the mountain tops.
Then up, up they went.
Parts of the Earth became icy cold.

Phaeton let go of the reins in terror.
He clung to the sides of the chariot.
Out of control, the horses went
   where they liked.
They went so close to the ground
   that parts of the Earth became deserts.
They went so high up
   that other parts became icy wastes.
Towns and cities were set on fire.
Forests and woodlands burst into flames.
Fields and meadows were scorched black.

From his sun palace, Apollo smelt
the terrible burning.
He feared that the whole Earth
would soon be destroyed.
Apollo called on Jupiter, the King
of all the gods, to help.

Jupiter shot a deadly thunderbolt
   at the sun chariot.
It hit Phaeton in the shoulder.
With his hair on fire, Phaeton fell to Earth.
Jupiter ordered the horses back to Apollo.
But Phaeton had fallen into a river.
Alas, he was drowned and his body
   was never seen again.

Cygnus, Phaeton's best friend,
   went to search the river for his body.
So long did Cygnus search
   that he was turned into a swan.
That is why there are on the Earth
   great hot deserts
      and icy cold areas.
And it is why, when you see a swan,
   you will find it looking sadly
      at the water over which it glides.

The precious jug

An old man wanted to go to the cellar
   to fetch some cider to drink.
He looked round for a clean jug
   but there wasn't one to be found.
'There's no clean jug in the kitchen,'
   he called to his wife.
'Then take the one from the china cupboard,'
   his wife told him.
  'But just you be careful.
  It's my best jug.
  I don't want you breaking it.
  And mind you don't go chipping it
   or cracking it.'
The old man couldn't do anything
   without his wife nagging him.
'Nag! Nag! Nag!' he said to himself.
  'Of course I won't break
   her precious jug!'

The old man started to go down to the cellar.
He did not see some bottles
   at the top of the steep steps.
The light was poor, and the old man
   kicked one of the bottles over.
It rolled in front of him
   and he stepped right on it.
His legs shot from under him
   and he began to fall,
      head over heels.
'I mustn't break the jug,' he thought.
So he twisted and turned and rolled
   this way and that way
      to keep the jug from breaking.
And he bump . . . crash . . . bump . . . crashed
   right down the cellar steps.

He hit the floor with a thud.
His elbows were skinned.
His back and his hips were bruised.
There was a lump on his head
   the size of an egg.
But the jug was still in one piece.

The old lady rushed to the top
   of the cellar steps.
'You clumsy old fool!' she cried.
   'Didn't I tell you to mind out!
   Didn't I tell you to mind my best jug?
   Didn't I tell you to be careful?'

Painfully the old man climbed to his feet.
Slowly he held the jug up high
    for his wife to see it.
'So you *didn't* break it after all?'
    she said in a pleased voice.

'No!' replied the old man.
 His body was aching all over.
'No, I didn't break your precious jug.
    But now . . . by . . . golly . . .
        I . . . WILL!'

Tattercoats

The lord of the castle sat by the window.
He shed tears of bitter sorrow.
He just sat and gazed at the sea
 and the lonely shore.
Day after day he sat there.
His beard grew longer and longer.
It grew down to the floor
 and wound round the legs of his chair.
His clothes became old and scruffy.
Nobody could comfort the lord.
Nothing would stop his sorrow.

A little girl ran into the lord's chamber.
She was as pretty as a picture.
Her skin was like a pink wild rose.
Her hair was as yellow as corn.
Her eyes were as blue as the sea
   on a warm summer day.
But the girl's dress was dirty and torn.
She had no shoes on her feet.
There was a black smudge across her face.

The lord of the castle stopped weeping.
He took one look at the little girl.
He clenched his fist and banged
   on the arm of his chair.
'Get out!' he screamed.
  'Get out of my chamber!
   Never let me see your face again!'

A servant rushed in.
She grabbed the little girl's hand
    and pulled her from the room.
'Tattercoats!' she shouted.
    'You know what your grandfather says.
    Never go to his room.
    Never ever let him see your face.
The servant cuffed the little girl,
    and smacked her legs.
A big tear ran down the child's face
    and splashed on the cold, stone floor.
'Get down to the kitchen.
    You'll find some scraps of food.
    Then get yourself to bed,' snapped the servant.
Poor Tattercoats!
Why did the lord hate her so?
After all, she was his granddaughter.
The lord once loved his wife
    with all his heart.
He loved his only daughter
    almost as much.
When his wife died,
    the lord was heartbroken.
Even so, he had his daughter to love.
Alas, she died too
    when she gave birth to a baby girl.
The baby was Tattercoats.
The lord hated the baby.
He never wanted to see her.
Tattercoats had no father
    so there was no one to love her.

The servants should have been kind
  to the little girl.
Instead, they treated her badly.
They laughed at her and teased her.
They called her Tattercoats
  for she had only one torn, ragged dress.
She had to be content with the scraps
  of food they gave her.
Most of the time she had to look after herself.

111

The years passed by.
Tattercoats grew tall and beautiful.
Her grandfather still sat brooding
  in his room in the castle.
The servants still had no time for her.
Tattercoats still had to be content
  with poor ragged clothes.

Whenever she could,
  Tattercoats wandered away from the castle.
She grew to love the wild sea shore
  and the woods and fields nearby.
She was never lonely.
Her friend was the goose-boy.
He had come to work for the lord
  on the day she was born.
Tattercoats loved to hear him play his pipe.
He would put it to his lips
  and play such sweet music.
She was sure his gentle tunes
  coaxed the geese to lay their eggs.
Often she was sure the birds in the trees
  sang to the goose-boy's sweet pipe.
When he played, she forgot the gloomy castle
  and her unhappy life there.

Tattercoats came home one day
　　to find the castle in an uproar.
Servants were rushing this way and that.
There was shouting and calling.
She had never known such excitement.
'Whatever's the matter?' she asked a servant.
'Nothing that concerns you,' said the servant.
Please tell me, someone,' Tattercoats cried.
She rushed from servant to servant
　　but they were all far too busy.

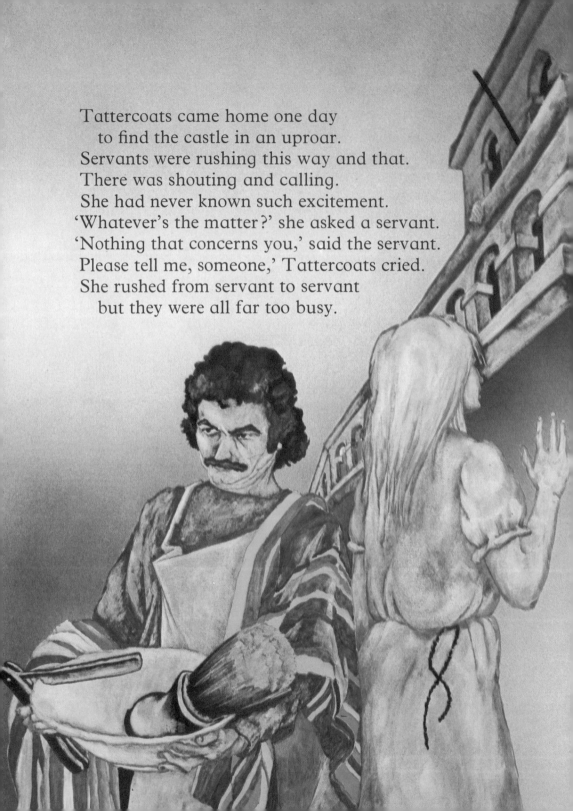

At last, she found her old nurse.
The nurse was the only one
   ever to show her any kindness.
'Haven't you heard, child?' said the nurse.
  'The King's son wants to marry
    but he can't find a girl to suit him.
Now the King is taking his son
   to every corner of the land.
Each town he visits is to give a ball.
Any girl who is well-to-do
   will go to the ball.
The King is sure that sooner or later,
   the prince will find a girl to please him.
Every important person is going.
Even your grandfather has been asked.'

'That is what all the fuss is about,'
   went on the nurse.
   'It is so long since the lord went out.
   His beard has grown too long,
      so he has had to send for the barber.
   His clothes are full of moth holes,
      so he has had to send for the tailor.'
'Do you think I will go to the ball?'
   asked Tattercoats.
   'After all, I am the lord's granddaughter.'
'What a silly idea, Tattercoats,'
   laughed the nurse.

116

Just then there was a roar
    from the lord's chamber.
His hair and beard were tangled together.
The barber could not help making
    the lord yell with pain.
'Please ask if I can go to the ball,'
    Tattercoats begged the nurse.
Another yell of pain rang out.
'It would be a waste of time,'
    said the nurse.

The next day Tattercoats crept away
    as early as she could.
She looked at her torn, ragged dress.
She felt her long, golden hair.
How she longed to go to the ball!
Then she saw the goose-boy coming.
The gay tune on his pipe made her smile
    and forget her sorrow for a time.
Later, the goose-boy said, 'Tattercoats,
    why are you so sad?'
So Tattercoats told him about the ball
    and the young prince who wanted a wife.
The goose-boy did not speak.
Instead, he put his pipe to his lips.
    and played a strange tune.
It was beautiful and tender.
It seemed to fill the air with magic.
'Come with me! Come with me!'
    the tune seemed to say.
The goose-boy moved away, still playing.
Tattercoats and the geese followed.
Soon they came to the road
    that led to the town.
Only then did the goose-boy stop his tune.
'Why have we come here?'
    Tattercoats asked the goose-boy.
But he held up his finger to his lips
    as if he knew a secret.
At that moment they heard a horse.
A handsome young man rode up.
He stopped beside them.

'Excuse me,' he said. 'I have lost my way.
  Can you tell me the road to the town
    where the King is staying tonight?'
Then the young man saw Tattercoats.
He felt he had never seen a girl
  so beautiful in all his life.
The goose-boy played on his pipe once more.
The music seemed to throb with beauty.
It seemed to weave a spell.
The young man got down from his horse.
He took the girl's hands in his.
'I cannot say how. I do not know why,'
  he said, 'but I love you with all my heart.
  Will you marry me?'

Tattercoats felt hot tears sting her eyes.
How could the stranger ask this of her?
He just wanted to tease her
   because of her torn, ragged clothes.
She pulled away and sobbed into her hands.
'Forgive me,' said the stranger,
   'but I see in your eyes the blue sea
      on a warm summer day.
   In your hair I see the golden corn
      blown by the warm wind.
   Your skin is like the sweet wild rose.
   I shall never find another girl like you
      if I live for a thousand years.'

Once again the goose-boy played his pipe.
'I ask only one thing,' said the stranger.
  'Come to the King's ball at midnight.
  Come in your torn dress and bare feet.
  Come with your geese.
  Bring your goose-boy to play
      his soft, sweet music.'
'She will be there,' said the goose-boy.
  And the stranger galloped away.

The ballroom was hot and stuffy.
The King tried not to yawn.
It was almost midnight.
The prince had danced with
  nearly all the pretty girls.
But he had not found one that pleased him.

The clock chimed twelve.
Suddenly, a strange sound filled the room.
It was the music of a pipe.
The band stopped playing.
The dancers stopped dancing.
Was that the smell of the sea
  and a golden cornfield on a summer day?
The King gasped in amazement.
A ragged girl came into the ballroom.
She had no shoes on her feet.
Her dress was torn and patched.
Behind her came twelve white geese
  and a goose-boy playing his pipe.

The King was about to shout angrily
but he could not break the spell
of the goose-boy's music.
It was so tender and beautiful.

The prince ran forward.
He was the stranger Tattercoats had seen
    on his horse that day.
He took Tattercoats by the hand
    and knelt at her feet.
'Father, this girl is more beautiful,
    even in rags, than any other.
She is the one I wish to marry.

Suddenly the room was filled with light.
Everyone was dazzled.
When they could see again,
    Tattercoats' torn old dress had
        become a beautiful gown.
She wore golden slippers
    and a necklace of gold.
The twelve geese had turned
    into twelve handsome page-boys.

Tattercoats married the prince
   and they lived happily ever after.
As for the lord of the castle,
   he just went back to his room.
There he sat brooding and brooding.
His hair and beard grew again
   and he never smiled.
As for the goose-boy,
   he was never seen again.

The hunter

A hunter once went into the jungle
   to look for the tracks of a lion.
At last, he came across a man
   carrying a camera.
'Excuse me,' said the hunter.
   'I'm looking for some lion tracks
      or even the den of a lion.
   Do you think you can help me?'
'Of course I can,' replied the man.
   'Follow me and I'll show you the lion itself.'
The hunter went pale with fear.
His teeth chattered and his knees knocked.
'W . . . W . . . Well,' he stammered.
   'I'm not really looking for the lion.
   I'm only looking for his tracks.'